For Louise and Eloise,
my inspiration and energy - J. L.

tiger tales
5 River Road, Suite 128, Wilton, CT 06897
Published in the United States 2016
Originally published in Great Britain 2016
by Little Tiger Press
Text and illustrations copyright © 2016 Jonny Lambert
ISBN-13: 978-1-68010-010-5
ISBN-10: 1-68010-010-6
Printed in China
LTP/1400/1242/0815

For more insight and activities,
visit us at www.tigertalesbooks.com

LITTLE WHY

by Jonny Lambert

tiger tales

At the back and in-between the Elders,

Little Why walked in line . . .

. . . well almost!

"Stay in line,
Little Why!"

Back in line,

Little Why spied Wildebeest.

"Wow!" Little Why gasped.

"I need some spiny-spiky special horns like those!"

"I would look super-duper scary!"

"I would charge this way and that!"

"Could I have some spiny-spiky special horns?"

"NO!"

"Why?"

"Stay in line!"

Back in line,
Little Why
spotted Giraffe.

"Oh, my!" Little Why
gasped.

"I need to get some long-lofty leggy legs like those!"

"I would be
super-stretchy tall!"
squeaked Little Why.

"I could reach the highest leaves!"

"I could see for miles!"

"Could I have some long-lofty leggy legs?"

"NO!"

"Why?"

"Stay in line!"

Back in line . . .

. . . Little Why spied Cheetah.

"Ooh! I want speedy-spotty, fuzzy fur like that!"

"Could I have some speedy-spotty, fuzzy fur?"

"NO!"

"Why?"

"Stay in line!"

NOT back in line, Little Why spotted Crocodile.

"Wow! What a snippy-snappy snazzy snout!
Could I have a . . ."

"Little Why,
you HAVE
to stay
in line!"

Back in line,
Little Why
sulked.

"If only I had fancy feathers,
I could flutter and
fly away like Bird.
If only . . . ."

"STOP!"

"Why?"

"Because . . ."

"...we're here!"

"You don't need spotty fur or spiky horns, Little Why. You have fantastic flippy-flappy ears, a super-squirty trunk, and . . ."

"... you're **special**
just the way
you are!"

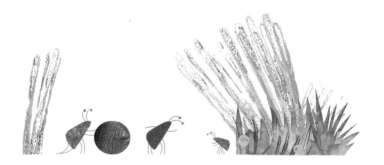